True Love's Kiss
A Supernatural Erotica

Chapter One

The Stranger

The drink in her hands could do little to warm her on a night like tonight. Her body was still chilled to the bone from the winter temperatures that continued to drop outside. A winter storm was coming, and it would make for unsafe conditions if she didn't leave earlier than she usually did.

There was time enough to worry about that. She still had a couple hours before she would have to head back out into the frozen world she was trying to escape. Hopefully, the liquor was able to break through the icy grip on her body and warm her by then. She hoped it would warm her spirits too.

This corner bar was a far drive from home considering the number of joints closer to where she lived. It had its appeal. No one knew her here. They didn't when she first started coming every weekend, sometimes twice depending on what she was dealing with in what she referred to as her real life. This place was fantasy. It was fiction. She could be anyone she wanted to here.

Scarlet chose to be herself. It was the only place where she could truly feel at ease in her own skin. At work, she was the trusted assistant, always prepared and ready for anything her boss threw at her with nowhere near the amount of pay or recognition she deserved. With her family, she was the wild one they wished would settle down. Friends thought of her as the victim who needed to find the one who would heal her heart.

At home, she was alone. She was left to her thoughts, fears, insecurities, and anxiety.

This bar let her be the person she'd been trying to become for years. She was the cool and collected brunette in the corner with green eyes that became more captivating with the makeup that highlighted them. They saw a quiet woman who kept to herself, but was friendly when approached.

In the months since she found this place, the regulars had gotten to know her a bit and welcomed her into their circle. They greeted her when she arrived then let her be alone in good company. Some of them would venture over for small talk from time to time. She welcomed it, but she wouldn't join them across the bar regardless of how many times they offered. She wasn't there to play pool, darts, or sit in a group telling jokes and reminiscing all night. All she wanted to do was pretend life was good for a little while before making the drive back to her empty one bedroom apartment.

It had taken several months for her to find a place far enough from her day to day where she could escape completely. There had been one other with potential. She had gone there a few times before anyone wandered in she recognized. That didn't stop her. She kept returning, but more and more, she knew some of the patrons. It stopped providing the same escape.

The other benefit of this small joint was the lack of men trying to get in her pants. Scarlet didn't have to travel this far to get laid. That's not why she was there. There had been a couple incidents where someone made a pass, but it was after she was welcomed in to the regular group. The first time it happened it didn't take more than a couple minutes before Gus, a big burly truck driver, had ventured over to make sure she was alright. She assured him the man was just leaving. It took one look at Gus for the uninvited stranger to get the hint. After that, she just glanced at the guys on the other side of the bar, and one of them came to take out the trash.

The day would come when someone would find her there. Technology made it impossible to hide for long. The one thing social media had taught her was that it really was a small world. There were co-workers who were good friends with people she went to school with, and the bad crowd she ran with during her rebellious phase knew the owner of her apartment building and her mechanic. It always amused her trying to figure out how these people who were so different in their lives had met and come to be friends. It was only a matter of time before some six degrees of separation connection ruined her bar for her.

Tonight, she wouldn't worry about the inevitable. It was time to relax and enjoy the limited time she had before she had to beat the snow and ice in the forecast to get home. There was no reason for it to occur to her limited time was all she had left.

The bartender was an intimidating middle aged man named Mongo. He got the nickname because of a deformity he was born with that made him look larger than life and like something straight out of Hollywood. If anyone made it past his jarring exterior, they'd find he was the most caring soul. He wrote tender poetry that could melt the coldest heart. Scarlet had read some of it he shared with her at the bar then sought out his blog to read everything as he posted it. He was good to her. She never had to order another drink; he always knew when she was ready and came over with another glass.

When the handsome stranger walked in the door, she expected Mongo or Gus to intercept before he made it to her table. It wasn't conceit talking. Aside from Frieda who was old enough to be her grandma, she was the only woman there. If someone was getting hit on, it would be her.

The man was incredibly handsome though. His looks were unmatched with his jet black hair, olive skin, and when he came closer, she saw his eyes were steel grey. It wasn't only his looks. He carried himself with confidence and class, and the way he looked at her sent a message of desire.

He walked directly to her table as soon as he entered. It was as if he expected her to be there and wanted to find her.

Scarlet couldn't remember having ever seen the man before. She was certain she wouldn't have forgotten his incredible good looks. It didn't surprise her that he'd make his way to the table of the only young single female in the bar, but it was alarming how he came at her like she had been there waiting for him all along.

"Good evening," he said. "Do you mind if I join you?" He pulled out a chair and sat down before she answered.

"Do I know you?" she asked. There was something about him that was familiar. It was like a scent or a song that takes you back to a place and a time that was better than the here and now. He stirred that sense of nostalgia in her, but somehow he was taking her senses back to him without even having met him before.

"You should," he told her.

The wheels started turning in her mind as she tried to figure out how she knew him. It had to be a very long time ago before he grew into the man sitting near her ordering a whiskey from Mango and requesting a refill for her as well. The only way she wouldn't recognize him now is if she knew him during his ugly duckling phase.

Mango brought over their drinks. His hands were trembling, and a few drops of mojito spilled over the glass onto the table. "I'm so sorry," he pleaded. Scarlet was going to tell him not to worry about it, but she noticed he was talking to the stranger, not her.

He held up his hand to stop Mango. "There is no harm done," he said, offering a very large bill to him. "Keep the change."

Scarlet sighed and pursed her lips. He wouldn't impress her by flashing his money like that. She had never been won over by a man's wallet. He was incredibly handsome and had money to burn. She knew the type, and she didn't want to waste her time in yet another controlling, mentally abusive relationship regardless of how sexy he was.

A dry smile formed on his lips, and he sipped from his glass. If she didn't know better, she'd guess he could hear her thoughts.

'Sexy? Where did that come from?' It shocked her to have that word enter her mind when she hadn't thought too much about him yet.

"Forgive me," she told him. "I don't remember meeting you." They needed to get the song and dance over with. He needed to hit on her, so she could turn him down. Then she'd head on home before the storm got too bad.

"Oh, that's not what I meant," he said, nodding toward her fresh drink.

As if he sent some subliminal command, she lifted her drink to her lips and took a long sip. Her heart began to race. The combination of being so close to him and his smooth, sultry voice was affecting her in ways she never experienced so fast and easy like this. "What did you mean?" she asked almost breathlessly.

"You *should* get to know me," he said, gazing deep into her eyes.

She gasped. Every negative thought she had about him, every red flag, and every warning alarm going off in her head was being silenced and pushed away. He'd been in the bar less than ten minutes, and she already knew she was his.

"Good. We're agreed," he said, standing up.

Scarlet didn't know what she had agreed to and narrowed her eyebrows together when she looked up at him.

He held out a hand to her, and she took it. Two minutes later, she was bundled up walking to his car in the parking lot, and she still hadn't even learned his name.

Chapter Two

Special Delivery

The next morning she awoke in her small apartment. Events of the previous night flashed through her mind like still picture images rotating at fast speeds. When she tried to focus on one to make sense of it, her head would hurt.

It was all very confusing. She wasn't hung over. There wasn't a massive migraine accompanied by the urge to rush to the bathroom to empty whatever may still reside in her stomach. The possibility of a date rape drug didn't seem likely both because she was too awake and alert. It was a mere twelve hours or so after the last thing she remembered clearly which was walking to a car with a man she'd only just met. Plus, she physically felt fine. The only issue was her lack of memory.

Scarlet rolled onto her back and sighed, hoping it would come to her. They left the bar together and went to his car where they made out for several moments while standing outside in the cold. He had kissed her suddenly which normally would've made her object. She wasn't typically one to move that fast.

His kiss had been different. It set off a chain reaction of excitement in her body unlike anything she'd ever experienced. The best way she could describe it in her mind would be like if all the sex she'd ever had was merely foreplay leading up to how this man could make her body react.

The stranger devoured her neck, gently kissing from one side to the other until his mouth pressed harder. His kiss became more demanding, more stimulating. There was a moment where she thought, and welcomed the idea, she would have sex with a stranger in full view of anyone passing by in that parking lot with freezing winds battering them. As soon as she expected him to start ripping off her clothes, he stopped and opened the passenger door of his car for her.

'*My car,*' she moaned.

It was still in the bar parking lot, almost an hour away. She had no idea what it would cost to be driven there, but she did know it was more than she could afford. Names started running through her mind of who she could ask for a ride there, but none of them were appealing. Either she didn't know them well enough to ask for such a sizable favor, or she didn't want to explain how her car came to be left at a bar so far away. They'd draw their own conclusions anyway.

That didn't take into consideration the storm that came through last night. It was supposed to dump over a foot of snow before morning with more snow in the forecast later today. The road conditions would certainly not be good enough to go after her car anytime soon.

'*Wait,*' she wondered. '*Is my car even still at the bar?*'

Scarlet stared at her ceiling as if she'd find the answer written there. She couldn't remember coming home. There was nothing concrete from the time she kissed a stranger until the moment her eyes opened.

Closing her eyes, she let the images flood in again, hoping to control them this time. At the very least, maybe one would clue her in to how she got home. It didn't work. She felt dizzy, and the room began to spin. When she opened her eyes, she was even more confused than she had been.

Her mind had to be mistaking last night with past movies she had seen or magazines she had read. There were pictures that made sense like seeing the strange man across the table from her in a fancy restaurant. She couldn't remember dining with him, but it could have happened. There were twice as many images that had to be wrong. She saw the Eiffel Tower from the perspective of someone standing at the base and looking up. She saw the Louvre, and not just the building's exterior either. There were memories of being inside the most famous art museum in the world after hours, being given a private tour.

Maybe it really was a date rape drug. Her mind wasn't based in reality anymore.

She pulled the blanket back and moved to sit up. Her body responded with various shouts of pain. This wasn't good. Her neck was sore, and it wasn't the type of sensation you'd get from pulling a muscle or strain from sleeping the wrong way.

Also, there was an intense ache between her legs. She hadn't noticed it until she moved, but it was a clear indication of having had some brutal sex last night. The acknowledgement began to creep in indicating the handsome man at the bar may have slipped her something, and she wasn't sure how to feel about it.

Of course, it was bad, horrible, and unthinkable. That was combined without having a memory of what happened. Yes, her pussy and inner thighs were letting her know someone, possibly more than one someone, had pounded her box into oblivion last night. She couldn't remember if it was consensual. She had no idea whether she should be upset, angry, hurt and scared or not, and that was what confused her.

She stood up slowly. Her legs trembled and shook under her

small frame. Oh, yeah. There had been some good sex last night regardless. Her body was exhibiting all the signs of multiple orgasms from a sizable cock.

There was a process that should be followed. Scarlet knew exactly what she needed to do, what she by all means should do. First, she needed to call the police to report it. Let them come and take a statement. She'd then be whisked off to the hospital to undergo a physical examination. In the end, she had nothing to give them. She couldn't even remember what kind of car he drove except to say it was silver. The police could question everyone who was at the bar last night to see if they knew anything, but that would ruin her relaxing spot she'd finally found. There would be no way she could go back there if they knew what happened to her.

'If they knew,' she thought. *'Hell, even I don't know.'*

Other than the evidence of sex and the literal pain in her neck, she felt fine. The rest of her aches were quickly diminishing. There wasn't much she knew about date rape drugs, but she knew they acted similar to alcohol in how they made you feel when you came to. That's why so many people figured they got blackout drunk the night before because their bodies responded the same way. If there had been a drug in use, she'd be hung over. If she had continued to drink after leaving with the stranger, she'd be hung over.

Scarlet walked into the bathroom and looked in the mirror. Last night's makeup streaked across her face. She turned the water on to begin cleaning it up when she noticed her neck. *'Damn!'* she thought. *'No wonder it hurts.'*

There was a hickey the size of a grapefruit on the right side of her neck. It was grotesque looking with its deep shades of purple and red. If she looked closely, it almost looked like there was a bite mark buried in the middle of it. She sighed. It would take a hell of a lot of makeup to cover that up for work.

She stripped off her clothes and turned the water on in the tub. Taking a shower would erase any evidence, but she had made up her mind not to report it. She wasn't even sure there was anything to report. Under different circumstances, she would make the call in a heartbeat, but there was something nagging at her. Some part of her was insisting nothing had happened without her consent.

After her shower, she wrapped herself in her robe, feeling much better all around. She had a long conversation in her head about what had happened. In the end, she decided she met a handsome man, continued to drink enough to black out most of it, but not enough to get hung over. She may have stopped drinking early enough or drank enough water before going to sleep to prevent feeling horrid today. Whatever the case, it was a lesson learned. She would never leave the bar with someone she didn't know ever again.

That left the issue of getting to work tomorrow. There was the subway and the city bus, but she didn't know the routes. She'd have to figure that out before morning. She headed to the kitchen to start a pot of coffee and eat breakfast. Then she'd tackle the issue of her car.

Nothing could've prepared her for what she saw when she came out of the short hallway from her bedroom. There were flowers everywhere. It was like her living room had been transformed into the local florist's corner store. At quick glance, there had to be over a dozen vases. Each one with an arrangement of various size, but all of them roses. There were individual roses dotting the room on the coffee table, laid across picture frames, and anywhere else they could be put. The floor was covered in petals as was her sofa and chair.

The counter in the kitchen that separated the two rooms had a giant teddy bear crammed on it. The brown bear was so enormous its head was down at a weird angle to fit in the large space. Next to it was the largest heart shaped box of chocolates Scarlet had ever seen. And, there were also more roses.

She walked through the room with wide eyes. It was one more thing she didn't remember, but something like this is usually left as a surprise. No one else had a key to her apartment. In fact, she didn't even have a spare.

Scarlet walked to the door, but all of the locks were set. One of the deadbolts matched the key to the knob, but the other could only be locked from the inside. It was more to add to the mystery.

Walking back to the middle of the living room, she circled around and around. This was the grandest gesture anyone had ever made toward her. Before this, she was lucky to get a card on any holiday. Even then, she would get it two days later after he found her secretly crying over being forgotten.

This definitely reinforced her decision not to call the police. If the worst had happened last night, her attacker would not have spent this much money on all of these flowers.

'*Money,*' she thought. '*A lot of money.*' For some reason, it triggered something in her mind, but she was still unable to recall exactly what.

As her eyes surveyed the room, she noticed something blue on the street from an opening in the curtains. She walked to the window, not thinking it was possible. When she looked out, she realized she was wrong. There was her car parked out front of her first floor apartment in her assigned spot. That solved the work issue, but she really wished she could remember driving home. She'd give it closer inspection after she got dressed, but from where she stood, it didn't appear to be damaged. That was good.

Scarlet was feeling better about everything. Even though she couldn't remember the details, it felt less ominous. She headed to the kitchen once again, but noticed a card attached to the largest vase that was placed in the center of the coffee table amidst several individual roses. She opened it and read it out loud.

"My dear, there is one rose petal for every time I've thought of you since we parted. Until we see each other again, we'll have Paris to keep us warm. Yours, Sebastian."

The card dropped from her hands to the floor. Her mouth fell open as images of the Eiffel Tower and the Louvre flashed once more in her mind. *'Paris?'*

Chapter Three

Do I Know You?

It had been almost one week since her encounter with the man at the bar. The soreness between her legs had lessened significantly. She learned that her inner thighs had actually bruised. It wasn't upsetting to see the bluish purple marks on her legs, but she did wish she could remember the sex that caused them. It must have been a hell of a ride. The bruises still bothered her sometimes when she moved just right, but that was it.

Her neck was a different story. The hickey had turned to a greenish yellow that was absolutely hideous. Between a fuck ton of make-up and styling her hair over it, she managed to keep almost everyone from noticing it. The people who did catch a glimpse didn't matter. They were cashiers and other people she passed on the street. No one who would recognize her as the hickey lady if they saw her again.

The people she worked with were the ones she worried about. It would be the hot topic of office gossip for a while, but it would never completely go away. It would take a very long time for her to live it down, if she ever did. If anyone at work saw it, they didn't say a word which told her none of them had.

She had debated about going back to the bar this weekend. Part of her was worried they all knew. Then she would have to ask herself knew what? Yes, they saw her leave the bar with him, but that didn't mean anything. He could've been someone she'd met years ago, her current boyfriend, a hot uncle, anyone really. They wouldn't know she left the bar with a stranger necessarily.

And, so what if they did? They were in no position to judge. She didn't know the others all that well, but she'd heard enough to be confident they had no right to belittle her for her choices.

Setting that worry aside, she had hoped they might help her figure out who he was. She didn't have the nerve to outright ask them. That would be admitting she threw caution to the wind and left with a man who was still unknown to her. Maybe they would give her a clue organically. She hoped when she walked in the door, Mongo might say something like, "Where's Sebastian? Figured he'd be with you again." She could then strike up a conversation with Mongo about the mysterious man she met. It was a long shot, but she wouldn't know unless she tried.

The only reason she was headed to her favorite bar on that Friday night wasn't just in the hopes of learning more about him. It was because she hoped he would return. If he didn't show tonight, and if she didn't get the answers from the regulars she needed to find him again, there was always tomorrow.

Scarlet felt an overpowering need to find him. There were so many questions about what happened that night, questions that only he could answer. She spent the week half expecting him to show at any moment. He obviously knew where she lived, and he cared enough to fill her apartment with roses and gifts. Who does that as a thank you for a one night stand? She had a realistic opinion of herself. Her pussy was good, but no pussy was *that* good.

These images that flashed through her mind confused her. It was like a puzzle with missing pieces and no picture on the box to guide her in solving it. The things she could see only added to the mystery. There was no way they had gone to Paris that night. It had been twelve hours, at the absolute most, from the time they left the bar until the time she woke up the next morning. Plus, she didn't have a passport. Unless he could teleport, Paris was out.

The way her pussy felt the first couple of days intrigued her as well. There had been some amazing sex between them, but she wished she could remember it. If nothing else, she wanted to find him just to have a round two.

It was more than any of that though. The draw she had to him was more intense than anything she'd ever felt. Something happened between them that night, something special. Her heart still felt the connection, but her mind did not. The need to find him could be felt deep in her soul.

She pulled into the parking lot and steered around to the side of the bar where she usually parked. It was the usual scene. Gus' pickup was already there. Frieda's old Corolla was parked right near the door. Mongo lived on the street behind the bar, so he walked to work. There were a couple other cars that she recognized as regulars', but she didn't know which belonged to who.

After she parked, she let the song finish playing on the radio before getting out. It wasn't because she wanted to hear the rest of it, but because she needed a moment to prepare for the lion's den she feared she may be walking into. Her nerves had her on edge even though she tried telling herself there was nothing to worry about. Even if they did think she hooked up with a complete stranger last weekend – which she did, it didn't matter. They weren't the type of people who went around judging others. She was an adult who could do as she pleased.

When the song ended, the DJ's voice came on the air and took the station into a commercial break. She turned the car off. It was time to face the music inside the bar.

Scarlet stepped out and shivered when the bitter cold hit her. She walked around the front of her car and kept close to the building as she went. The parking lot still had scattered patches of snow, and she didn't want to slip. When she rounded the corner of the front of the bar, she saw him.

Parked at an angle in the middle of the lot was a familiar looking car. The man standing next to it had been hazy in her mind when she tried to recall him during the week, but she recognized him immediately now. It was Sebastian, a name she only remembered from the card she'd read multiple times a day since Sunday.

The smile that formed did so on its own, and she walked straight to him. "Do I know you?"

"You should," he replied.

There was a thin space separating them now. She could smell his scent under his cologne. Her body was responding to his presence, and she had to use restraint not to wrap herself around him. "Forgive me," she said. "I don't remember meeting you," she teased. The repeat of their first conversation was fun, but it was also not far from the truth.

"I was afraid of that, my love," he said, placing his hands on her shoulders and gently kissing her forehead. "I promise you won't forget me again."

The words he used were lost on her. She didn't pay attention to how odd it sounded like he somehow magically erased her memory. All she focused on was his touch which heated her near frozen body, and his lips which left her wanting more.

"Shall we?" he asked. "I was beginning to think you'd never come."

"Me?" she laughed, allowing him to open the door for her. "I arrived first."

He closed the door and walked around to the driver's side. After he climbed in, he turned to her, and said, "Yes, but I thought you may never get out of your car."

Scarlet was in a trance. All of her questions escaped her. There was nothing that seemed off about the way she just fell back in sync with him. She was merely content to be near him once more. Her body relaxed so deeply she hadn't realized how tense she had been. It was like not being with him set her on edge, but now everything had been righted.

The atmosphere inside Sebastian's luxury car was intoxicating. It would be hard for Scarlet to describe how it felt being near him. There was a calm, peaceful feeling. It assured her that everything would be perfectly fine now that he was there.

She was always burdened by the struggle of her own life with bills that kept growing, a past that still haunted her, and a few jerky male co-workers who thought her role at their company was for their visual enjoyment. They made sure to never say or do anything that crossed the lines of sexual harassment. It was nothing that could be proven, but it didn't change the way they made her feel. All of that along with her own insecurities and doubts washed away just being close to him.

It was also sexually stimulating. From the moment she first saw him standing in the parking lot, she could feel her heartbeat in her clit. The air between them was ripe with their pheromones. If it weren't for the slick, snowy residue on the roads leftover from last weekend's snowstorm, she would have unbuckled herself and leaned over to start kissing his neck, letting her hands roam over his body. The threat of a wreck prevented her from doing it. That, and he looked like he might be too classy to allow such behavior.

Sebastian chuckled, muttering something under his breath.

"What was that?" she asked.

"Nothing," he said smiling.

Scarlet thought she had heard him say, *I'm not. I assure you.* She knew she had to be wrong. He couldn't be a mind reader.

"Would you like to go back to my place first?" he asked. "We can decide how to spend our time together from there."

'Or maybe he was,' she thought.

"Yes," she told him, a little too eagerly. "I'd like that."

He drove through the city to the winding road on the edge of town that led to the wealthy homes that sat on the hillside, overlooking the hustle and bustle below. It was giving her a sense of déjà vu even though she couldn't remember having been there before.

Sebastian pulled up the circle drive of his large mansion and parked. He came around to Scarlet's door and opened it for her. When she stepped out, he pulled her close and kissed her. The freezing wind had just begun to sting her skin when his lips touched hers then she melted and felt the fire swirl inside her.

She followed him into his home, both not recognizing it and having a vague feeling she'd been there before. A butler met them at the door and took their coats, asking how long they'd be staying. "I'll let you know, Morris," Sebastian said. They continued to talk for a moment.

Scarlet didn't hang around. She walked down the hall to the right to a bathroom. In her mind, she knew it was the smallest bathroom in the house even though it was over twice the size of the one in her apartment. She wasn't sure how she knew that little detail any more than how she knew where the bathroom was located.

After she freshened up, she joined Sebastian in his den. Once again, her feet guided her as if from muscle memory, but she felt like she was seeing everything for the first time. With her hand on the door of the den, she closed her eyes and pictured it in her mind. There were floor to ceiling bookshelves on three walls. The fourth wall was mostly filled out by large windows. Near the back of the room was his mahogany desk where he was likely sitting, drinking a cognac. She walked in and looked around, gasping. She had been wrong, but barely. He wasn't sitting at his desk, but standing, drink in hand.

There was a current of excitement that ran through her when she saw the look in his eyes. She was all too aware he desired her just as much, if not more, than she wanted him.

He handed a glass out to her, and she walked over to take it. "What's on your mind?" he asked. "I'm afraid something troubles you."

"Why can't I remember?" she asked.

Sebastian wrapped one arm around her waist and pulled her tight to him. "That would be my fault, my love," he whispered, kissing her gently. "I was too eager with you last time. I promise you won't forget everything tonight."

It was like a riddle she heard a hundred times even though it was new. It was both puzzling and understood, but she sensed the answer was there in the part of her brain that was locked. She would know what he meant if only she could recall their last meeting.

"What would you like to do this time?" he asked. "Paris again? You did enjoy it so."

Scarlet laughed. This she knew had to be a joke. Perhaps some secret only the two of them shared. "We didn't go to Paris," she smiled at him lovingly.

"No?" He raised his eyebrows. "Then we should go again if you've forgotten," he said, pushing off the desk and walking her back a couple steps. He circled his arms around her waist and began to sway to music only he could hear.

Two could play at this game. "Italy," she said, challenging him. "Venice."

Sebastian stopped dancing and stared into her eyes deep enough to pierce her soul. "Beautiful choice," he said. "The trip may frighten you, so you should sleep."

She started to object. She was intoxicated by the feelings that enveloped her. There was not a chance she could go to sleep. He leaned in and kissed her while continuing to gaze into her eyes, and he didn't remove his lips from hers until she was out.

Chapter Four

Venice

When she opened her eyes, she was alone in the king sized bed, but it didn't alarm her. Scarlet knew Sebastian would return. The hotel suite was large and exquisitely decorated. He had spared no expense on her. She crawled out of bed and didn't think twice about being completely nude even though she had no memory of coming to this room, much less taking off her clothes.

There was no ache between her legs this time. Nothing had happened the night before. Part of her was upset he hadn't touched her, and part of her was hoping he would soon.

Through the open curtains of the windows, she could see the buildings huddled closely together spread out across the landscape. While she couldn't see the ground from where she stood, she knew if she walked closer to peer below, she would see canals instead of grass. This was Venice.

The thought entered her mind as a truth, not something to guess. Her last memory was of being in his den with him, yet somehow she knew. Those questions wouldn't riddle her mind until next week when she was back in her normal day to day. How did she know where she was? How were they able to get there so fast and her without a passport?

She hadn't been awake long and was considering taking a shower to get ready for the day, but she didn't know what the day would entail or how to prepare. There was a knock on the door while she was deciding what to do.

"Room service," a man's voice called out from the hall.

She grabbed a robe that was hanging near the bathroom and yelled, "Come in!"

A man in a crisp black and white uniform entered the room, pushing a full table ahead of him. He asked her where she'd like to have it put. Scarlet pointed over by the window in the sitting area of the suite. It would be nice to look at the picturesque scenery while she ate. He arranged a few things on the table then turned to look at her again before leaving. "Will there be anything else?" he asked.

Her purse was setting on a side table, and she walked to it, fishing through it for cash to tip him. She was unsure of what amount would be appropriate.

"There's no need," he told her. "The gratuity has already been paid."

The man left, and she made her way to the spread that had been delivered. There was everything she could possibly want, ham and cheese omelet, bacon, sausage patties, hash browns, French toast lightly dusted with powdered sugar, and a bowl of assorted fresh fruit. There was even a boat of sausage gravy. She couldn't make up her mind, so she fixed a plate with a very small portion of everything.

Sebastian walked through the door after she had barely begun to eat, carrying a garment bag. "You're awake, my love," he said, smiling at her. He laid the bag across the back of the sofa and bee lined to her. He leaned down and wrapped his arms around her from behind, kissing the sides of her face and neck gently. "How is your breakfast?" he asked.

She swallowed the bite of syrup drenched French toast she had in her mouth, and told him honestly, "Delicious. Join me," she offered happily.

"No, my love, I'm fine. This is for you."

"There's so much to choose from," she giggled. "I could never eat all of this."

"Yes, I wasn't sure what you'd be in the mood for, so I ordered all of your favorites," he explained.

The thought that hit her was, *'Of course you did.'* It seemed natural like this was something Sebastian was known for, something he had always done. It never occurred to her that this was a man she barely knew and had only spent two evenings with. For the life of her, she could not recall ever discussing favorite foods with him. Those thoughts wouldn't creep into her brain until mid-morning on Tuesday when she was losing the battle of staying focused on her work.

He sat at the table near her and gazed out the window for a minute before asking, "What would you like to do first?"

Scarlet really had no idea where to begin. Venice had its appeal due to the gondola rides in the canals. Other than that, she really wasn't sure what all it had to offer. "You mean you didn't plan anything?" she asked, teasing him.

"Oh, I have planned a dozen different versions of how we could spend the day, but I want to make sure we do whatever is in your heart to experience."

"As long as I am with you," she told him, "that is all that's in my heart."

He took her hand and kissed the back of it. "When you're finished, I've picked you up something to wear," he told her. He nodded toward the garment bag he had carried in with him.

"There are three outfits for you to choose from since we left in a hurry and forgot to pack."

She laughed like it was an inside joke that was theirs alone. She finished her breakfast and rushed off to get ready. The clothing he picked out was stylish and expensive. It was hard to choose what to wear, but she picked the most relaxed of the outfits, not sure what the day would entail. If she needed to, she could change into a dress later for dinner.

The day whisked by in a breeze. Sebastian took her to St. Mark's Basilica and Square. She was impressed by how well he spoke the language. They drifted through the canals on a bridge tour. They watched glass workers, and he bought her a small hand crafted piece as a souvenir. It cost more than she made in a month.

When evening rolled around, he took her to a small restaurant tucked away in an area that had to be known only to locals. The food was divine. She had never had anything so delectable in her life. Then they walked, hand in hand, back to the hotel. It was quite a trek, but it seemed to go by in no time with him by her side.

Inside their room, the sparks begin to fly immediately. It was like they had both been pushing their physical desires aside the entire day to enjoy Venice, but once the door shut behind them, it was the signal to let their carnal urges loose.

Scarlet walked into the bedroom, knowing Sebastian was right behind her. She placed one hand on the bed's post to balance herself while removing her shoes. The warmth of his arms engulfed her, and his mouth found the other side of her neck from where he had left his mark last weekend. The pressure hardened, and she pulled away.

"Whatever is the matter, my love?" he asked.

With her hand covering the place where his mouth had just been, she told him softly, "Don't." She tilted her head to expose the other side of her neck. The discoloration had faded, but it was still there, covered by the makeup she had applied. "I'm still sore from the last one," she said.

He gave her that smile that melted her so easily and approached her again. He placed his hands on the side of her face and kissed her gently. "That is my fault," he admitted. "I didn't heal you. I wanted it known, to be seen, that you were taken. It was wrong of me. Can you ever forgive me?"

She nodded and smiled at him. "Yes," she said, lifting her mouth to meet his. There was nothing he could do that she couldn't forgive because it was him.

Sebastian kissed her passionately then brought his lips to her neck once again. "Do you trust me?" he asked.

"Yes," she whispered.

There was a brief moment of pain when he kissed her neck again, but it was quickly followed by pure bliss. The love and desire she felt for him swelled within her until she believed her heart may burst while she orgasmed from a kiss.

He pulled his head away and gently laid her down on the bed. Scarlet suddenly felt a little tired and weak, but he did everything as if he already knew she couldn't. He undressed her gently, kissing each part of her body as he revealed it. When he let the last piece of her clothing hit the floor, he loosened his tie. He stripped down deliberately, not putting on a show, but with heated intent while staring into her eyes.

Sebastian slid one arm underneath her and guided her up into a better position, one where she was fully supported in the middle of the bed. He hovered over her, taking in her nude body as if it was the first time he had laid eyes upon it. Slowly, he kissed down over her breasts, onto her abdomen, until his mouth found her sweet spot between her legs.

The sensations his lips sent through her were unparalleled. Scarlet arched her back and grinded her hips into him. There were sharp little nibbles that sent her into higher waves of ecstasy. No one had used their teeth on her like that before, and now she wondered why the hell they hadn't. It was the perfect blend of pleasure and pain.

He brought her to climax faster than any man ever had, and she came hard. Her entire body shook. He didn't remove his mouth until she had completely finished, relaxing into the bed, gasping for breath.

Sebastian crawled up on top of her with a devilish smile on his face. He centered himself between her legs, gently nudging them apart. "Ready for more, my love?" he asked.

She nodded still out of breath.

"Say it," he commanded.

Scarlet took a couple more breaths, and managed to say, "I'm ready."

"For what?"

She propped herself on her elbows, bringing her face closer to his. "I'm ready for you. I want to feel you inside me. I need your hard cock inside me."

The grin on his face grew, and he touched his forehead to hers. He pressed gently, pushing her head back on the bed while he came down on top of her. Then he pierced her tunnel with the tip of his stiff shaft.

There was a sudden intake of air when he entered her. His

size was massive. She managed to sneak an eyeful while he had undressed and knew he was the largest she'd ever had, but seeing it and feeling it were far different. Now that he was thrusting into her, she felt like her pussy was being split to accommodate his girth and was sure she couldn't take his full length.

Scarlet came twice before she felt him grind against her. She lifted her head and looked between them. He was fully buried within her tunnel, and she gasped.

"My love," he moaned. He stared deep into her eyes until his gaze seared her very soul. "You are the home I've been looking for all these many centuries," he said softly.

His words sounded poetic, albeit nonsense. Sebastian didn't look a day over 30, maybe 35. Still, she understood him. It was like lifetimes of existence had to play out perfectly for the two of them to find each other.

When he came, she came with him. Their bodies were one, but it was more intense than anything she had ever felt. Fleeting images passed through her mind while her pussy contracted around his shaft, and her cum flowed out between her legs. They were foreign to her like she was seeing what was in his mind. That's how connected they were in that moment.

Chapter Five

Under the Weather

Monday morning rolled its ugly head, and Scarlet got ready for work. Once again, she couldn't remember arriving home, but she could recall more of the weekend this time. Pieces of it floated around her head while she went through her morning routine. Her hand instinctively went to her neck, expecting it to react with violent pain to the touch, but it didn't.

She looked in the mirror, but there was no mark. That was one thing she knew for certain. Sebastian had kissed on her neck hard, hard enough to hurt. The memory was hazy. She could remember that it did happen, but couldn't remember it happening. The other side of her neck had fully healed as well. There wasn't a mark to be seen anywhere.

Their weekend was all she could think about as she drove to work. More details seeped through. The images were on a high speed flash show behind her eyes, and it took effort to pause on one of them to recall the specifics. The sex was most vivid. If there was to be only one thing that stood out vivid in her memories, her brain had selected correctly. Scarlet had never experienced sex that good.

Throughout the day, random thoughts would hit her from nowhere. How did they get to Venice? She didn't have a passport. When she had asked Sebastian about it, he said he flies privately. It had been taken at face value over the weekend, but she couldn't help but question it now. Even people with private planes still have to abide by rules, laws, and regulations, especially internationally. Wouldn't there still be customs to go through? Scarlet didn't understand how it was possible, but he was the one with the private plane, not her. He should know what he's doing. Yet, if she was going to continue to see him, she should get a passport just in case.

There was something else that riddled her. As hard as she tried, she couldn't remember being on his plane at all even though she had flown in it two weekends in a row. No matter. She had probably slept through the flight.

'*Two weekends*,' she thought. The words popped out at her. She had spent two weekends with him for a total of three nights. She still didn't know his last name. While she could find his house again if she wanted to without the actual address, she didn't know his phone number or how to get ahold of him. Scarlet didn't even really know if she'd see him again except she *knew* she'd see him again. She wondered if he had told her as such and made plans that couldn't be found in her foggy mind.

The memories were too cloudy. She didn't remember drinking, not more than a few glasses of wine. It couldn't be the alcohol that caused her to be so fuzzy.

Whenever these questions popped up, and they did often, she would start to realize nothing made sense. Two and two definitely weren't adding up to four. As soon as an alert crept over her that something about Sebastian and their time together was off, she'd be filled with a peaceful calm that told her everything was fine. He was her one and only, and they would see each other again soon.

By the end of the week, she had caught some bug that she

figured must be going around. She didn't really feel sick, not in the traditional understanding of most illnesses. Something was wrong with her stomach. There was an almost constant gnawing hunger. The hunger was extreme like she hadn't ate in days. Whenever she tried to eat something, no matter what it was, it would make her sick to her stomach.

It had been there all week but got worse after lunch on Wednesday. They had a food day at the office. Her boss had burgers and wings brought in from a local place, and the staff had signed up last week to bring in side dishes and desserts. She assumed when her stomach started acting up worse than it had that it was something she ate.

After spending a noticeable amount of time in the bathroom that afternoon, she felt better, but it was brief. She had barely got back to her work after playing twenty questions with her boss about whether or not she was okay and if she should go home before the hunger began. This wasn't the typical eat lunch at noon every day, but now it's half passed one where your body knows lunch was delayed. This was severe cramping and growling that co-workers two cubicles away could hear. She felt weak and unsteady on her feet like she could pass out at any moment. It literally felt like she'd gone days since her last meal. It was the worst hunger she'd ever felt, but even that was temporary. With each passing day, it became more and more intense.

She went back to the tables that had been pushed against the wall, covered with generic dollar store tablecloths that were already filled with holes and ripped. Some of the food was gone, either because it had been finished off entirely, or the person who brought it in had stored it away to take the leftovers home. There was still plenty to choose from, but she was careful with what she grabbed.

Prepared foods would be the worst choice as you couldn't be entirely sure how safe it was. She stuck to the store bought options. There was one bag of plain chips and a veggie tray still unopened. They looked to be the safest bets. She added some baby carrots and a few pieces of broccoli, skipping the dip because she didn't think it wise to try dairy, and she poured about a handful of chips on her plate then took it to her desk.

When she bit off a bite of carrot, her stomach started singing her praise. It was about time she gave it what it had been demanding. The gratitude didn't last long. She hadn't swallowed the entire bite before it was clear she needed to rush to the bathroom again.

This time her boss sent her home. It wasn't out of any concern for her, but rather because he didn't need whatever she had to spread to the rest of the office.

Scarlet stopped by the grocery store on her way, picking up foods she thought might be safe to eat. She grabbed anything soft with little to no flavor. Toast or crackers had been what her mom always gave her when she was a child, but they wouldn't work now. As soon as she started chewing, the gag reflexes would begin. It had to be foods that could just be swallowed with minimal effort on her part.

It didn't take long after returning home for her to discover that what she bought wasn't going to do the trick. Even Jell-O had the same effect on her. She was miserable. Usually when she's sick, her appetite disappears. This was new. She had never had an illness where her body rejected every possible source of nutrition while punishing her for not providing sustenance either. The pain from her hunger was unbearable.

The only thing she could keep down was water. Her body had no reaction to it whatsoever. Eventually, she found the courage to try coffee, and it was the same. Soda, however, was a no go. She could swallow it without issue, but once it hit her stomach, it was game over. There was a little apple juice in her refrigerator, so she gave it a try. Her body yelled at her for it, but didn't reject it.

She could drink. There were certain liquids that her body didn't object to her consuming. The milk in the refrigerator remained untouched. She still knew better than to attempt dairy.

Scarlet found the energy to drive back to the store. The whole drive was spent thinking about what drinks she could keep down that might be able to provide some nutritional value. Smoothies could be an option if she made them carefully, selecting ingredients that would be the least harsh on her system.

The cart kept her upright while she wandered the store. She leaned on it for support like an elderly woman substituting the cart for her cane. Aisle after aisle, she scanned everything hoping to find a solution. Finally, she saw one. There was no guarantee it would work, but it couldn't be any worse than what she'd already experienced. She grabbed a six pack of creamy nutritional shake substitutes. There were three flavor options to choose from, but she stuck with vanilla to be safe. It gave her another idea, and she headed off to the infant section for an electrolyte solution.

Back at home, she tried the drink designed for babies and toddlers first. It had to be a gentle formula given who was meant to be drinking it. There was some uneasiness, but it wasn't bad at all. She could keep it down, but it wasn't filling. The hunger wasn't going anywhere. The supplements had been put in the refrigerator when she got home, but they wouldn't be cold yet. She still tried one. It was a little rougher going down, but she was able to manage it. These ones didn't give her the feeling of being full either, but at least they had nutritional value. She poured one into a large bowl and put it in the freezer. One long hot shower and two sleeping pills later, she pulled it out and ate it with a spoon. It tastes like generic subpar ice cream, and she managed to keep it down too. She had to eat it slowly, putting it back in the freezer a couple of times before she finished it. The pills started to kick in when she was done, and she happily laid down. When she was asleep, she wouldn't have to deal with the pain this bug was causing.

At least that's what she thought. In the morning, she woke up from the strangest dream. She had flown down over two people on a jog. The hunger she felt was so severe she tore into their flesh to satisfy it. The hunger was still there when she woke.

The next two days at work were torturous. She stocked up on the supplements and poured them into her travel mug at work. As long as she didn't try to chew anything, she could manage. The growls from her hunger weren't completely silenced by the nutritional shakes, but they did quiet down some.

When quitting time rolled around on Friday, she considered not even going back out to the bar. At the start of the week, she had planned on going again on Friday just like last weekend. This way she could have two chances of running into him in case he wasn't there tonight. She was so weak from the lack of food, she considered giving it one more day. By tomorrow, she might be feeling better finally.

The desire to see Sebastian again won over. She came home from work and immediately began readying herself to go out. It took her twice as long to do even everyday tasks, so she needed the head start. Looking in the mirror, the image staring at her didn't match how she felt. There was a young, vibrant beautiful woman staring back at her, but she felt like someone with one foot in the grave. She locked up and headed down the stairs. What happened next was a complete surprise.

Chapter Six

The Staircase

Sebastian was double parked directly in front of her building, standing next to his car looking handsome as ever. A warm glow filled her body as soon as she saw him which temporarily made her forget about how ill she had felt the last few days. "I have a surprise for you," he teased.

She walked up to him until they were inches apart and placed her hands on his chest. "Perfect," she said softly. "I love surprises."

He leaned down and kissed her. The passion swelled within, and she felt an ache build between her legs. She hoped the surprise was staying in this weekend because she was ready and eager to stay in the city at his house instead of travelling to anywhere extravagant again.

That was her last thought before waking up in a bedroom that was foreign to her. She wondered briefly how he was able to do this, how it was that her memory was so affected when she was with him, but as soon as the thoughts formed, there was the familiar nagging in the back of her mind like it had all been explained. Everything was as it should be.

Sebastian appeared in the doorway like he sensed she had returned to life. "My love," he said. "How was the trip? You're not too tired, I hope."

There was something about his presence, his very essence,

which melted her and put her at ease. "I feel well rested. Thank you," she said, bringing herself to his embrace once again.

He wrapped his arms around her, pulling her close. "When you are ready," he said, nodding to the dresses hanging in the open closet. "I'll be waiting." He took her hand and gently kissed the back of it before leaving the room.

Scarlet floated like she was on a cloud, making her way through the bedroom suite to the most beautiful bathroom. It was bigger than the living room of her apartment and more exquisite than she could imagine. Everything reminded her how lucky she was to find someone like him. Love and money didn't often collide, but in their case, they had.

She showered, pampering herself with the product available to her to take her pick. The shampoo alone probably cost more than she earned in a day. When she was almost finished getting ready and sat to slip on her heels, Sebastian appeared once more on cue.

"Shall we, my love?" he asked, extending his hand.

He helped her up and kissed her gently before leading her into the hall and down a grand staircase.

"Where are we?" she asked.

Sebastian tilted his head and furrowed his brow with real concern. "You don't remember?"

She shook her head.

"This is one of my properties," he said. "It's an ancestral estate. I have some business that requires my attention, so I need to be here this weekend." He stopped at the bottom of the stairs, making sure she kept her footing on the old stone floors. "No matter how far I travel or how successful I become, it seems I must always return home."

It sounded like music to her ears. *'Home.'* She had an apartment. It was where she lived, but there hadn't been a place that felt like home to her for far too long. He hadn't completely answered the question. He hadn't told her they were in Romania. They could've as easily been in England or Scotland, but she didn't catch how he intentionally left some of the details out of his reply.

He led her into the dining room which was laid out for a romantic dinner for two, and pulled out her chair. "I know you wanted to stay in this weekend, my love," he said. "You can stay in here. I hope that suits you."

Of course it did. Everything Sebastian arranged for her was perfect. Did he know she wanted to stay in? She couldn't remember telling him of her desires, but she couldn't remember getting into his car either when she obviously had done so.

A man dressed like something out of a fairy tale from the past entered through a side doorway, carrying a tray. He ladled a delicious smelling soup into the bowl in front of her, but it made her stomach flip. In an instant, she was reminded of the bug she'd been fighting.

"Still feeling under the weather?" Sebastian asked.

Scarlet felt horrible, and she really wanted to taste the soup. The aroma was enticing, but painful at the same time. The hunger that had escaped her since awaking a short time ago returned with a vengeance. "Yes," she admitted. She lost track of how many details he seemed to grasp without remembering having ever told him.

"Have a drink," he smiled. "It'll settle you right away."

The glass in front of her had to be hundreds of years old. It was a rather plain goblet, but she could tell by the design it was an antique. She lifted it and looked inside to see what it held. It looked like wine, so she took a sip. For the most part it tasted like wine except for a slight metallic taste which she figured was caused by the makeup of the goblet.

It worked immediately to ease her upset and even the screams of starvation from her stomach ceased. She had never heard of wine being used for medicinal reasons other than sedation, but this was better than any medication she had tried.

Sebastian's eyes twinkled, and he chuckled softly. "Your surprise amuses me," he said.

"I've tried everything to rid myself of this stomach bug," she confessed. "I would have never thought to try wine."

He nodded and tasted his soup. "It's from my family's vineyard," he said.

Nothing he said amazed her anymore. Of course his family had a vineyard. It sounded as natural as discussing the weather.

While the intense hunger had dissipated, the fact remained that Scarlet hadn't ate a decent meal since breakfast Wednesday morning. That's if you count a yogurt eaten in the car on the drive to work as a decent meal. She devoured what was in her bowl down to the last drop of broth.

"I know you're famished, my love," said Sebastian. "Take it easy. You don't want to create a different kind of upset."

Scarlet felt embarrassed until she looked at him. That was all it took for a calming sensation to wash over her. The connection they shared was more intense than she had ever imagined could be possible between two people. She was safe with him. It was a feeling she was experiencing for the first time.

For the rest of the meal, she ate carefully, enjoying every bite. The flavors were more robust than what the fanciest restaurant back home served. Each individual spice could be detected by her palate, and they danced on her tongue to a symphony created by the dish as a whole. Sebastian spoke of having to return to this home almost as if it was something he didn't enjoy, but she hoped to come here again and often. If not, she would attempt to persuade him to move this chef to the house in the city.

When their meal was finished, he took her hand and led her into a small sitting room, asking her if she'd like a drink. She didn't mind having one, but she refused. There was something else she wanted even more.

"It's late," she teased. "I think it's time to head to bed."

"Bed?" he asked surprised. "You've only just awoke, my love." He saw the look in her eyes and realized what she really meant by her choice of words. "Oh, I see."

Sebastian walked to her and gripped her arms firmly as he held her close, crushing his lips to hers. When he pulled away, they began walking toward the old stone staircase. Each of them unable to keep their hands off the other.

By the time they were halfway up the stairs, Sebastian was half undressed, and everything Scarlet wore under her dress had been discarded. He wrapped a hand around her waist and lowered her to the cold stone step. "I've been longing for this since we last parted," he said.

Standing a few steps below her, he knelt and buried his head under her dress. Scarlet's hand flailed in the air until it found the railing to hold onto for support. Her other hand braced over the edge of a step, and her head rolled back while moans broke free from her lips, unable to conceal them.

He worked his tongue expertly around her clit while slipping a finger inside her, then two. He fucked her with his digits while lapping at her outer folds and circling her clit, occasionally nibbling gently with his teeth. Scarlet was cumming within minutes.

She pressed against his shoulders until he finally leaned back and looked at her. "I want to feel you, Sebastian," she said softly.

Sebastian stood and helped her to her feet. He unfastened his pants before lifting her up, and she wrapped her legs around him. He turned and balanced her against the curved wall of the stairs. It was an awkward position without the imbalance of standing on two steps at once, but he managed it flawlessly. With one arm around her to hold her steady, his other hand worked to free his massive hard on from his pants.

"I need to be with you again, my love," he whispered. His cock touched the entrance of her tunnel, and he pushed his way inside.

The sheer girth of him caused her legs to tremble and the walls of her pussy to contract around him. A steady torrent of her cum ran over his cock and down her legs. He plowed into her relentlessly until he began to grunt and buck as he shot his load.

Once he had her back on her feet, he kissed her slowly. "Now, let's go to our room where we can do this right," he said, leading her up the rest of the way.

She hated to see the weekend come to an end. It was harder to say goodbye to him, but now the dread of having to end the weekend Sunday night put a damper on their time together. Before he left her on the steps of her building, he handed her a small flask, telling her to think of it like it was medicine with instructions to add a shot to her coffee every morning. Doing so would ensure the stomach ache, and all the problems it brought with it, would not return.

Chapter Seven

Severance Package

Throughout the following week, Scarlet no longer had disrupting thoughts about Sebastian. Nothing he did seemed strange any longer. The holes in her memories which only occurred when she was with him didn't make her pause. Everything seemed normal to her, and the fact that it actually wasn't normal for anybody else had escaped her. Those moments of clarity were gone. All of the details that did pop into her head would spark red flags for everyone, but not her.

If she had more close relationships, these would be pointed out for her. An intervention might be staged to save her from him. The lapses in memory and giving her a wine made from his family's vineyard as treatment would send obvious signals she was being drugged even though a blood test would show nothing of the sort in her system. The grandiose display he showed, flying her to foreign lands, the lavishness of his many homes, and extravagant hotel rooms might seem like too much and carry the hint he was deceiving her.

After all, no one can fly to Italy and back inside of one weekend without a passport and have time to explore. It's not possible. It has to be directly linked to the drugs he's slipping to her. The hallucinogenic side effects leave her believing an illusion. Anyone trying to prove it would be left with more questions than answers, but none of this would come to pass.

The job she had was just a means for survival. The work itself wasn't bad, and the pay was great. There was a handful of coworkers she could do without, two in particular. They made her work day miserable. Instead of focusing on the tasks at hand, doing her business, and clocking out, she spent too much of her time keeping an eye out to avoid them as much as possible.

She's had a lot of practice and had become quite good at it, but she was distracted with thoughts of Sebastian and longing to see him again. The weekend was too far away. That's how she almost bumped straight into one of them returning from the break room where she had refilled her water bottle.

Derrick blocked her path, joking about where was the fire. He rambled on to her about a project he was working on and basically touting how it would fail if it wasn't for his keen eye and quick thinking. He was always boasting about himself like he truly believed he was as awesome as he hoped others thought him to be. The entire time he spoke his eyes rested on her breasts.

This had been going on since her first day with the company. No amount of reporting did any good without witnesses to his behavior. "Derrick," she said. The disgust she felt for him spilled out in her voice when she spoke his name. "Eyes up."

He glanced at her face and laughed before returning his gaze to her chest.

"I mean it," she said loudly. This time she was loud enough for a couple others to hear and assertive enough for them to make their way over to see if there was a problem. It wasn't out of concern for her, or anyone, but it was a desire for office gossip.

Derrick placed his hand on her shoulder, giving it a quick squeeze. "Calm down," he said. His creepy smile accompanying his words.

Scarlet raised her arm and swatted his hand off. "Derrick, I've told you I do not like you touching me."

He cried out in pain and reeled against the wall. He cradled his arm, holding it close to his body.

The scene he was causing infuriated her more. It was okay for him to take liberties and touch her whenever he wanted, but when she stands up for herself, he acts like he's the victim. It was for the benefit of the people who had showed up to see what was going on. As he continued to make a fuss, more people trickled into the hall. It added fuel to his performance, and his theatrics increased.

Management got involved, and Scarlet found herself explaining her side of what happened to HR. They accused her of attacking him which was utter nonsense. All she did was swat his arm away, and she repeated that over and over.

There were witnesses to what happened, and luckily, they made the same statement. Derrick touched her, and Scarlet brushed his arm away. It was not forceful or violent. Their recollection of it was the only thing to save her from being fired outright if not also facing a police interrogation.

Derrick insisted the pain was severe and went to a medical clinic to be examined. His shoulder had been dislocated. It was hard for her to believe when she was given the news two hours later, still sitting behind closed doors with the human resources manager. An explanation was expected from her, but she had none to give.

There was no way this was caused by her because she didn't have the strength necessary to do it. There were witnesses who backed up her version of events. He touched her, and she swatted his arm off her. That was it. Period. It didn't add up. Maybe he had a pre-existing injury that set his arm just right for this to happen easily. This was the only defense she had because she knew she wasn't capable of dislocating his shoulder under normal circumstances.

It wasn't enough for HR. The reasoning behind how it could be possible for his shoulder to be dislocated from such a small contact didn't matter. It happened nonetheless, and it was something that needed to be addressed and handled properly in a way that would be satisfactory to all parties involved.

Scarlet was sick of the bullshit. She had made reports on Derrick multiple times and nothing was ever done, not just him but Jason too who was almost as bad. The entire time she sat in this office they talked like she was the problem. No one else had ever reported them. It was only her, and now one of them was injured. The common factor was Scarlet. It became obvious she was losing her job today, and if that was the case, it was going down on her terms.

The job meant nothing to her, so she switched gears. Instead of continuing to defend her actions, she began to negotiate her resignation. When she walked out of the office over an hour after everyone else had left for the day, she felt good about how it worked out.

She had a lucrative severance package that was more than enough to sustain her while looking for another job. The letter of recommendation was all accolades about her performance for them. While there was no question this wasn't the right place for her, she couldn't help but feel a little depressed on her way home. On paper she left voluntarily, but she knew the truth. It made her feel like a failure.

Her apartment building came into view, and she debated

about going home right away because she didn't want to be alone with her thoughts. There wasn't anywhere else for her to go really. She'd be alone wherever she was regardless of how many other people were there. It would be three full days until she saw Sebastian again, and he was the only one she wanted right now.

She parked and walked up to her building, not paying attention to her surroundings. For the first time, she wished she had his phone number, but she did know where he lived at least. She felt dirty like the events of her day had tainted her somehow. A shower was a must, and maybe afterward, she'd develop the courage to show up at his house unexpected.

When she opened the door to her apartment, her eyes were on the floor while she fished her key out of the door. She kept her eyes lowered coming down the hall to the open kitchen and dining room. Her mind was so cluttered with her poor pity me thoughts she didn't realize she wasn't alone until she heard his voice.

"My love, why do you look so sad?" Sebastian asked.

Scarlet's entire frame lifted with the rushed intake of air after seeing him. The smile that formed couldn't have been stifled if she tried, and she walked straight to him. The question of how he entered her apartment never formed in her mind.

He took her into his embrace and comforted her. "That place was beneath you," he said. "You know it's true."

She did in a way. Whether or not it was beneath her was up in the air, but she had never been happy there. Once again, the question of how he already knew she had lost her job escaped her. "It still makes me feel horrible whether I deserve something better or not," she said to his chest, breathing in his scent.

"That's why I am here," he told her. "To cheer you up!" He

gently moved her back and placed his hands on either side of her face. His eyes penetrated hers, staring into her soul. He gave her a brief yet passionate kiss, and she forgot everything else in her life, the world, except for him. "Where would you like to go, my love?" he asked.

Nothing came to her right away. "I don't know," she confessed. "You pick."

"Where haven't you been?" he asked out of politeness. He knew her answer before she said it.

"Everywhere," she laughed. "I never even left the state until we met."

"Hmm," he smiled. "Maybe we should stick closer to home then. How about New York?"

Chapter Eight

The Decision

New York City was more magical than any of the international destinations he had taken her to, more than all of them combined. The lights were so sharp and focused. There were colors here she hadn't remembered seeing anywhere else. The sounds, and the noise which never stopped mind you, were both overwhelming and singularly impressive. It was as if time stopped regularly allowing her to hear the honking of a horn, shouting of pedestrians, thuds coming from shop owners setting up displays on the streets, dogs barking and more, as individual audio detections even though they occurred at the same time, or they could run together in a tidal wave of city orchestral accompaniment if she chose.

They dined at the finest restaurants. The food was so sublime she could taste the ecstasy on her tongue from the aroma that drifted off the plate when it was set down before her. When she finally brought a bite to her lips, her entire mouth dance with electric reaction to the flavors.

New York City gave her a feel of fantastic tourism destination and home at the same time. If she was single, she'd fancy moving there, but Sebastian would have to stay near his work she presumed.

They spent as much time in the hotel room as they did enjoying the city. Scarlet could spend the rest of her life in his arms and never long for more. His appetite for her was just as massive, just as unending as hers was for him, perhaps stronger.

On Sunday evening, he took his time with her. Sebastian stripped her down slowly, covering her entire body with his mouth. He tasted every bit of her.

When he laid her back on the bed and buried his face between her legs, the passion within her overflowed quickly and repeatedly. He was skilled with his mouth like no man she had ever met, like nothing she ever imagined possible. Each flick of his tongue, each suckle on her clit was deliberate and timed to meet her emerging climax. He could bring her closer, or hold her on the brink of release. She was at his mercy.

Many orgasms later, too many to keep count, he lifted his head, and asked if she wanted more. "Yes," she moaned breathlessly.

Sebastian rose up and climbed onto the bed. He got on his knees between her legs and brought his upper body down over top of her. "Tell me if it's too much, my love," he whispered. "I don't want to hurt you."

Experience had taught her there would be marks tomorrow. Her inner thighs would be bruised, and her entire pelvic area would feel like it had been crushed. She knew she would heal because experience showed her that too, and she was recovering faster each time they were together. Her body was adjusting to the blissful onslaught making love with Sebastian entailed. It would be another week or two before she made the connection to the healing flask he gave her when she was sick and had refilled for her this weekend.

He leaned closer, and she felt the tip of his shaft press gently against her downstairs lips. He paused, and she lifted her hips up in invitation.

A smirk drew up one corner of his lips, and he said, "I want you too, my love." He pressed farther, and she felt him enter her.

Every time they were together, his size impressed her. His hard cock forced its way into her tunnel, spreading her open more than she had ever experienced. The size of his member alone was enough to trigger her climax.

He inched his way in slowly until his full length was buried in her labyrinth. Then he pulled back and thrust into her hard.

Scarlet's moan escaped harshly, almost sounding like a scream.

"Are you okay, my love?" he asked.

She moaned over the sheer sense of being stuffed, and ordered, "Don't stop."

Sebastian obeyed, and repeated the move. He pummeled into her pussy repeatedly and without relief.

Her tunnel contracted around his cock, squeezing on to him, trying to prevent him from pulling back to no avail. Her love juice flowed freely, covering his shaft and running out of her, down her leg, and soaking the sheets where they joined together. The orgasms didn't stop. They ran together like the most intense, record breaking orgasm she ever had. Sebastian continued to drive into her, slapping his body against hers hard enough to move her across the bed, until her head which had been near the middle of the king size mattress was hitting the head board on his third stroke.

He pulled her back and wrapped his arms around her shoulders, holding her in place while he thrust, hard and fast into her, picking up speed each time. Soon he was fucking her hard, and she didn't notice the cries of pain from her legs over the assault they were taking. A lone, sharp cry emitted from her lips constantly while her body twitched from the never ending climax.

When she thought she couldn't handle anymore, she stayed quiet. She couldn't ask for it to end, but his timing was impeccable as always. Sebastian let out a growl which signaled he was close, and with one last thrust that hit so hard she wondered if he wasn't trying to fold himself inside of her, he came.

As she lay in his arms in the afterglow, she began to think to herself about if she even wanted to go back home. She certainly didn't have to right away. While Sebastian's schedule was still unknown to her, she could easily take an extra week of doing nothing but spend what free time she had with him before she'd have to get back to her reality.

Sebastian read her mind once more like he was becoming known to do. "The choice is yours, my love," he told her. "I want you to take your time before deciding. Think it over. Think everything over thoroughly then do it again."

"What's there to think about?" she asked, snuggling closer to his side. Scarlet was referring to her growing love for him and desire to stay with him always. When he first responded, she wasn't sure if he understood what she meant, but he had.

"I'm being serious. I shall have you home by morning, and I want you to take the week, longer if needed. You can give up your old life and come with me. I long to have you by my side for eternity," he whispered into her hair.

It made her smile hearing him use the word eternity. That's how she felt about him as well. She wanted to be his for all time, not just the confines of their lives.

"If you're not ready, my love," he adjusted his position to

look her in the eyes, "I'll wait. For you, I've waited a hundred lifetimes, and I will continue to wait until you're ready."

She gazed into her eyes, and the corners of her lips turned up in the beginnings of a smile. The exhaustion she felt from the sex they'd had and the climaxes he brought her so easily was taking over, and she was drifting fast. "Everything is you," she said, closing her eyes and succumbing to sleep.

Sebastian wasn't sure if it was a slip of the lips from her tired mind, or if she was ready, if she felt as he did. For he realized the moment he first laid eyes on her everything was her.

Scarlet spent most of the next several days eagerly awaiting for Sebastian's next visit. She couldn't wait to tell him she was ready. It was all she could do to stop herself from packing until the day finally came. She knew it was important to him that she give this a lot of thought which was what stopped her. If he didn't think she had carefully considered his offer, he might not take her, not right away, and she couldn't endure the time apart from him again.

Whenever the urge came over her to prepare for her move, she'd force herself to stop and think about a life with Sebastian, if that was what she wanted. The answers came to her before the questions were formed in her mind, but the fantasies of what their life together would entail kept her distracted for hours. By Thursday night, it wasn't enough anymore. She needed to see him, and even the grandest fairy tale her mind could concoct wasn't enough to prevent her from casually cleaning out a cabinet or throwing some items into a box.

If their history served as any indication, Sebastian would be here tomorrow. Scarlet only needed to make it through one more day before her new life would begin, and she decided to go for a walk. It may not help her to focus her attention on actually weighing this decision like he wanted, but it would stop her from packing her apartment at least temporarily.

She wandered the city streets with no real direction as to where she wanted to go. Several businesses she passed by multiple times with no memory of repeating her steps because she was lost in her own little world, a world where only the two of them existed. They were the stars, the highlights, the only ones that mattered, and everyone else were background characters, serving only to move the plot, their plot, along.

Hours after she left her apartment, she found herself in a neighborhood park that covered the entire city block. Two walkways covered the park diagonally meeting in the middle of a giant X. She zigzagged her way through, covering both decorative walks and the sidewalk that surrounded the park entirely. As she walked, she became vaguely aware of a couple arguing on a park bench.

They were older than her, probably in their late 30's. Scarlet had no desire to eavesdrop on them, but it was clear they were upset. They were the only three people in the park at the time, and she kept a safe distance to give them their privacy, but made a second lap through the park out of curiosity.

There was something about the couple that drew her to them, and it took a while to figure it out. In fact, she couldn't get them off her mind even after she returned home. They were still at the forefront of her thoughts when she laid down to sleep. It wasn't until the morning when she understood why she had been so fascinated with them. The thought was in her head as soon as she woke up.

It had been a normal couple in the park having an argument.

Something tugged at her deep inside telling her what she had with Sebastian wasn't normal. There was a brief, almost eluding clarity over it. Nothing about their relationship was customary, but she didn't understand why. She went over every detail she could remember of their time together until he arrived that evening, but nothing stood out as odd. Even the idea that many of their first memories were muddled or lost to her didn't strike her as unusual anymore.

Chapter Nine

Vampire

Scarlet was in her bedroom, tidying up Friday afternoon. Not knowing what was in store for her, for them, only what she desired. It was better to be safe than sorry, and she didn't like coming home to a dirty apartment. No one would ever refer to her home as dirty even on her worst days, but she wanted to have everything in order nonetheless.

A strange sensation moved through her, and she stood tall near her bed. All of her senses were on alert like some sound or scent would clue her in to something that had happened or was out of place. He was here. She didn't know how she knew, didn't know what tipped her off to his presence, but when she walked down the hall from her bedroom, she knew she'd find him waiting for her. How he managed to enter her apartment was a question she once again failed to realize should be answered.

"My love," Sebastian greeted, holding out his arms to her as soon as she appeared.

Scarlet went straight into his arms, pulling him tightly to her. Every stress she had been experiencing floated away which was an easy feat since almost all of it was caused by being away from him.

They kissed passionately, and she tore at his shirt, wanting him to take her right there on the living room sofa. He gently moved her away. "Have you given it any thought, my love?" he asked. "My proposition?"

"Of course I want to be with you!" she cried out, smiling at him with a heart so full of love it was ready to burst.

He chuckled and tucked the loose wisps of her hair behind her ear. "As I you," he said. "Have you given it *thought*?"

"Yes," she answered.

Sebastian led her to the sofa to sit down. "Then let me answer your questions," he told her.

She hadn't prepared any. When she tried to come up with them on the spot, the only one she found was living arrangements, but of course, she would live with him. It would be absurd to give up his beautiful home and sprawling grounds to move into her apartment. "There was a couple at the park," she said, drawing on the only thing coming to mind. "They were different, and I understood that really it was us who are different. I don't know why."

"I was afraid of this," he said after a moment. "Let me help you."

"The reason your memory was spotted after we first met is because I fed on you without healing your wound," he explained. "The open wound gives me time to flee without being tracked, not that I needed to run from you. It was careless on my part."

Scarlet listened to him as if this was an everyday occurrence most couples experience.

He continued, "When we traveled to far off locations, you flew in my arms. There were no private jets as you imagined. That's why no passports were needed. I made sure you were unconscious for it to prevent you from succumbing to your fears, and afterward, I erased memories before and after the trip to be sure you retained nothing."

This puzzled Scarlet. There was an idea desperately trying to grasp hold in her brain that people can't fly. It never quite gained traction, so she was left with the feeling this shouldn't make sense without knowing why it didn't.

"Your strength has been increasing because I've continually fed. If the feeding stops, you will return to your normal self soon enough, but for now, you're transitioning. The hunger that consumes you isn't a human construct, although it feels quite similar. The hunger you feel is the need to finish the transition, and once it's complete, it will be the hunger that drives you to remain as you have become."

"What transition?" she asked. It was the only word that popped out to her from all that he had said. This was the only word that her effected mind couldn't make sense of enough for her to ignore.

"The transition to become like me," Sebastian said, taking her hands and kissing them gently.

There was a brief moment of joy because Sebastian was her sole focus followed by confusion. The idea was to be with him, but she didn't understand being like him. "What are you talking about?" she asked.

Sebastian looked deeply into her eyes, and said, "Don't be afraid, my love."

It sounded silly to Scarlet because she could never be fearful of him, but she didn't realize he wasn't merely voicing his concerns. He was issuing an order that she would have no choice to obey.

He opened his mouth slowly, pulling his upper lip back in an unusual formation. His expression was quite comical, and she almost laughed until she noticed his teeth. The upper cuspids in Sebastian's mouth were growing. They elongated until at least twice their original size and sharpened to points at the end. The matching teeth on the bottom had grown as well coming to a point, but she hadn't yet spotted them.

There was no fear. Her instinct was to reach out and touch them which she started to do, but he grabbed her hand. "Careful, my love," he said. "They are extremely sharp."

The way he spoke had changed. His voice was different, almost accented. It was from the change in the makeup of his mouth which she couldn't remember having seen before now, but the sound of his voice, this version of it, was sparking a memory she couldn't load.

"That's right," he told her. "You've seen the real me on many occasions."

"Who is the real you?" she asked, feeling like the words weren't her own.

"What, not who," he corrected. Sebastian bared his fangs one more time before they disappeared, and his teeth returned to normal. "I'm a vampire," he said.

"And my transformation?" she asked. For the first time since she met him, things were actually making sense, clicking in her head, instead of feeling like there were holes in her mind.

He nodded, "That's right. It's to become one as well, but the decision is entirely up to you. It can't be forced, or rather, I won't force it on you."

"How do I complete it?" Scarlet asked.

"You have to drink from me," he said.

She looked at him with a thought she could almost grasp, and he saw the question in her eyes. "Yes, my blood. You have to drink my blood then it is done."

"What happens to me if I don't?" Scarlet's mind was becoming clearer by the second. She couldn't remember where they dined the last time they were together or what she had ordered, but this she could comprehend.

"That depends. There are options, my love," he told her. "We can remain as we are, but we may need to add space between our meetings. Your strength has become rather impressive too quickly. We can't have you breaking someone's hand with a high five. There would be too many questions."

"Also," he went on, "your memories of our time together will always be dodgy."

Scarlet looked away. She didn't like the idea of seeing him less, and she definitely didn't want to continue to forget details of what little time they shared together. "You said there were options," she pointed out. "What are my other choices?"

"There's only one more, my love," he said softly. "I can stop feeding on you, and you can return to living a normal life."

'Why didn't he lead with this one?' she thought.

"But I'd have to erase your memory of me completely," he added. "I know you would promise to keep me a secret, but it's too much of a threat to me, and my kind, to risk it."

That wouldn't do. The thought frightened her, and she flinched back away from him. She'd do anything to stay by Sebastian's side. Without him, her life was tedious at best, and she couldn't bare the idea of living her mundane existence, not having him to shine light on her world. Even if she wouldn't remember him, wouldn't have anything or anyone to miss without the memories, she couldn't do it because the person she was right now, in that moment, loved him too much.

"It's only one option, my love," Sebastian soothed. "I wanted to make sure you were aware of all of them, but the choice is yours. I will do nothing without your permission."

It didn't feel like much of a choice to her. One path led her to find another thankless job where she'd have to put up with more Derrick's of the world. She'd be passed over for promotions and recognitions because upper management liked to keep the workers busy and promoted the ones who wasted company time. There'd be bills, illnesses, weather that delayed her, irritated her, and made it difficult to drive. All of the annoying aspects of life awaited her. The only comfort would be Sebastian, but she wouldn't remember most of the time they shared together.

On the other hand, she could leave everything behind and be with him for eternity. There was much left unknown about what it would entail, but she would remember every experience they shared. It would only cost her an appetite for blood and her soul. It was tempting to agree to it immediately. "Do I have to feed on humans?" she asked.

Sebastian chuckled softly. "No, my love. It is not required in today's age. There are other ways of obtaining blood which you will need to consume for your body to survive. Feeding on humans is left to those who do it for sport, or to control someone, or in our case, when they've fallen in love with one. My love for you makes you irresistible to me which makes it impossible to refuse your taste."

Scarlet looked around her apartment at everything she would leave behind. There was nothing she would miss. "Let's do it," she said.

Chapter Ten

Nature Rendezvous

It had been almost a month since Sebastian sent a crew to her house to pack up everything she owned which wasn't much. Most of it was donated. Only her sentimental items were brought with her to her new life with Sebastian. He sold the beautiful home he had near where they met, and they embarked on a new adventure.

They had been traveling the world for weeks, going to every destination her heart desired. He called it their honeymoon even though they weren't properly married and wouldn't be. A paper trail wasn't wise when you needed to be able to disappear easily.

It wouldn't be long before they chose a place to start fresh. They would buy a home and live together under the false pretense of being a married couple until they had to move on before questions about their youthful appearance that never seemed to age started circulating.

There were things she was learning about him, and what to expect for her, and how vampires lived. Most of them were no different than any other person you passed on the street except the persona you saw was a cover. Blood kept them alive, kept them young, and strong. They could fly, but didn't turn into bats like some of the old myths claimed. Garlic was a welcome addition to any meal just as churches, crucifixes, holy water and sacred ground held no magical properties against them.

Sex with him had always been tiers above what she had experienced in her past, so it was quite a shock when it improved far better after her transition. He had been holding back to avoid hurting her. It could've been so much worse than bruises on her legs. In fact, he could've accidentally killed her if he didn't hold back.

Once she transitioned, she discovered how primal, how earth shattering the sex could actually feel. On their travels, they found outdoor locations to sneak off to for their urges because nothing had survived his bedroom before they put his house on the market. They had broken every piece of furniture, knocked every painting to the floor, contents of the dresser were strewn about, and doors had been shaken from their hinges. It looked like it had been ransacked when they finished and surveyed the damage hours after they began.

Their new home would have a room for them to explore their wildest needs without worry of damaging anything. It was an enticing promise that she fantasized about every time her mind was allowed to wander. She enjoyed their outdoor adventures, but it would be nice to have a place where they were constantly staying alert for anyone who might be heading their way before someone stumbled upon them in the act. Aside from all of the regular reasons to want to avoid an unplanned audience, it would be difficult to explain how they were having sex against a tree fifteen feet off the ground without support. For now, they enjoyed their walks in nature, going off trail to get as far from spectators as possible.

Sebastian stopped at a random spot surrounded by moss covered trees. The gentle tug on her hand told her he was no longer moving by her side. Scarlet looked back into her lover's gaze and walked into his arms. It was dusk and soon the cover of darkness would aid in their camouflage. He leaned in to kiss her, pulling back at the last second before doing it again, teasing her.

She interlaced her fingers on the back of his head and pulled him close, holding him still while she brought her mouth to his. Their lips locked together, and her passion swelled within, leading to a gentle throb on her clit. The one thing she would never tire of was making love to him.

Kneeling before him, she unfastened his pants revealing his already stiff member. She took it in her hands and brought the tip in her mouth, moistening it with her tongue, and slowly wet his entire shaft before bringing it to her mouth to begin sucking gently. She took it in little by little, bobbing up and down on his cock until his entire length was in her mouth and throat. She'd have never been able to take him entirely before her transformation, but could swallow him fully now.

He tilted his head back and groaned. It was music to her ears, encouraging her to continue, faster with each time she swallowed his cock. She was careful not to graze him. Things were different with her newly sharpened teeth. Even without transitioning to vampire form, they'd slice his flesh easily. Healing wouldn't take long, but it was still an uncomfortable situation she wanted to avoid putting him through.

After several minutes, he gently pulled on her shoulders, lifting her up. Once she stood in front of him, he spun her around and lifted her skirt, reaching one hand between her legs. His other hand fondled her breasts. He leaned close to her neck. His hot breath increasing her response and gently nibbled on her ear. "My love," he whispered. "There are not enough hours in the day to explore you."

His words melted her, and her knees buckled. Sebastian gripped his arm tighter around her upper body. "You like that?" he asked.

"Yes," she moaned.

He bent her over and positioned himself to enter her from behind. She reached out for something to brace herself, and he chuckled.

Sebastian entered her slowly, thrusting his full length inside her. He continued to fuck her with a soft rhythm, gently increasing until Scarlet was at her brink.

She realized her feet were no longer on the ground, and her arms instinctively flailed out around her. It was a sensation Sebastian assured her she'd grow used to, but she wasn't so sure about it. This time her hand hit the trunk of a tree, and she applied pressure with her palm, holding them in place. It was hard to tell in the evolving darkness how far they'd traveled. Their first night experimenting outside took them halfway across the state.

He pounded into her harder and harder while she kept them balanced against the ash tree. He drove his cock into her without reservation of if her body could handle it. These weeks since she'd drank his blood had been bliss while he could let his passion and desire run untamed. She was close. He could feel her body tense as it prepared to rain cum around his shaft.

Scarlet moaned out loudly as her orgasm rocked through her body. It was heightened now as was everything. Her tunnel clenched on him tightly and could hold him in place if she focused on it. Sparks flashed under her eyelids, and when she opened her eyes, streamers of purples, reds and golds floated around them in the night sky.

To her surprise, Sebastian pulled out when her climax ended. They would need to change positions, possibly head back near where they started and begin again. "Where are we?" she asked.

"The perfect location," he replied. "We're miles from the nearest people, my love," he said.

Scarlet smiled, but was too breathless to giggle. "Are you accusing me of being too loud?" she asked, aware her voice had been known to echo off the trees and carry far away from wherever they may have snuck off.

"I'm saying you will be," he said.

There was a tone in his voice, indicating he was up to something. It was playful, and she loved it when he was like this.

"Oh, I will?" she asked, challenging him. The last time he mentioned the volume of her moans she stayed intentionally quiet for several days when they fucked. It took a lot of willpower and was only accomplished because she bit through her lips. Her teeth ripped them to mesh, but they healed before he could see the real damage done.

"Yes, my love," he said, spreading her open to get into position again. "I've been wanting to do this since we met."

"Do what?" she asked.

The words had barely escaped her mouth when she felt the head of his cock push against the tight hole of her ass, and she gasped. She'd never experienced anal before and quickly tried to compute the likelihood and extent of damage a vampire could cause against her rapid healing rate. This was going to hurt.

"Is this alright?" he asked, pressing slightly harder against her opening.

Scarlet felt her hole try to widen in preparation, inviting him inside. "I've never," she said, unable to finish the sentence. She was completely unworldly in every way compared to him.

"I know," he said. "I'll be careful."

She smiled. Sebastian would never hurt her. She was safe with him always. "Okay," she said. "Let's do it."

"Oh, my love," he moaned affectionately. He pushed into her harder, and entered her ass.

Scarlet felt like she might split in two. The pain was sharp and intense, but then it subsided. Sebastian pulled out and entered her again several times. Each time, the pain was at its worse for the first few seconds. Once he got a rhythm going, he began slow deep strokes until she could feel his body hit against her ass cheeks. He was completely inside her or at least close to it.

Her moans were practically screams. The sensation of having her ass crammed with his cock was pleasing, but the noises leaving her mouth grew louder as he continued. Sebastian reached around and played with her clit which only increased her pleasure.

He slammed into her hard, again and again. The walls of her pussy convulsed and her juices ran down her legs constantly. A month ago this would've surely killed her. The power behind each of his movements tore into her. The pain was surpassed only by her pleasure. She placed her free hand over the one already resting on the trunk of the tree and discovered her hand had actually dug into the trunk by a couple inches.

Soon a low growl could be heard behind her, and she knew he was close. He shot his load into her ass. The molten liquid warmed her all through her abdomen. When he pulled out, he swirled her around to face him and crushed her mouth with his.

"My love, that was wonderful," he said, struggling for breath.

They held each other several feet off the ground. Both of them panting and trying to regain control of their breathing. When they could speak again without pausing after every spat out word, he suggested, "Are you ready, my love? Shall we go back?"

"No," Scarlet said. Her eyes twinkled. "In a few minutes, I'll be completely healed. Let's stay for another round."

Coming Soon

Kindle Vella

Family Secrets #4: Abby's Night
Nightwalker
Deadly Sins: Pride
Nanny Diaries Box Set

More by Darling Coxx

The Nanny Diaries Series

All five installments of this series are now available! Follow the journey of five young women trying to make their way in the world who have taken jobs as live-in nannies. These books are their diaries. Read about the adventures they had taking care of their own needs. Check them out if you dare! Darling Coxx's writing always scratches the itch you can't reach on your own.

Family Secrets: Lexi's Education

Lexi had lived a sheltered life thanks to her step-dad. He was a good man, a good, muscular, handsome, type of man. One thing he made sure of was that no one took advantage of his gorgeous step-daughter. Soon she'd be off to college in another state where she'd be at the mercy of the boys she met on campus. She needed a different type of education, a sexual education, and her step-dad was the right man for the job.

Family Secrets: Tiff's Fantasy

Tiff's life was far from perfect when her mom wrecked it even more by moving the man she was about to marry and his son into their home halfway through senior year. Connor was not a complete stranger to her. She'd known him all throughout school, and the fact he was about to officially become her step-brother was a nightmare. The most popular boy at school and the least popular girl under one roof. The only thing that could make it more complicated was her fantasies about him and his attraction to her.

Family Secrets: Natalie's Secret

Natalie's life kept taking one bad turn after another. When her step-brother Eli left for college, she was forced to fend off her newest step-brother Zach alone. It didn't take long until she realized Zach wasn't as bad as she originally thought. She tried to keep their affair secret, but Eli found out. He wasn't upset about it for the reasons she expected. Eli was jealous. There was room for both of them in her life and her bed, but they weren't the only pseudo family who had eyes for her as she would soon discover.

About the Author

Darling Coxx is a seasoned writer who has been featured in many major publications under her given name. Taking a break from interviews and personal experience pieces, she is trying her hand at short novellas in the same genre she's been working in for most of her life.

Her adult entertainment career began while working as the manager of an adult store. It is her favorite position of any she's held, before or since. It was there where she made the contacts that allowed her to venture into the world of adult entertainment both in her own writing as well as producing a few pieces of her own.

Please feel free to reach out to her at DarlingCoxx@gmail.com. Follow her on Instagram @DarlingCoxx to stay updated on future publications.